Fairy Tale Science

Making a Windproof House for the Three Little Pigs

by Sue Gagliardi

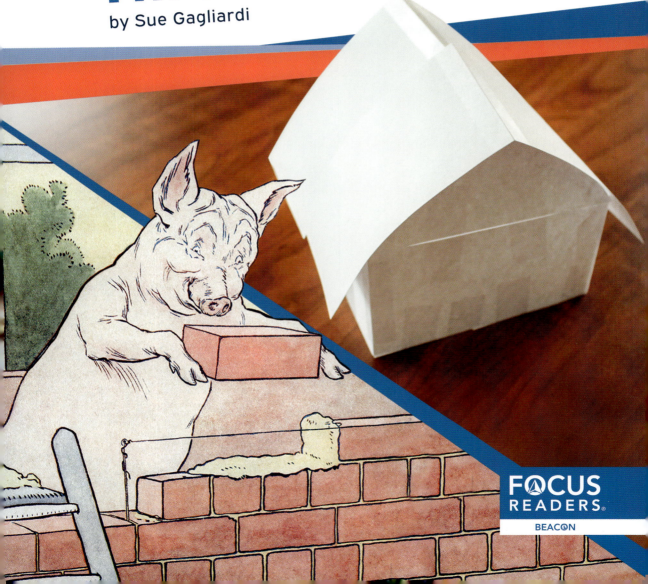

FOCUS READERS

BEACON

www.focusreaders.com

Focus Readers is distributed by North Star Editions:
sales@northstareditions.com | 888-417-0195

Produced for Focus Readers by Red Line Editorial.

Photographs ©: Lebrecht Music & Arts/Alamy, cover (left), 1 (left); Red Line Editorial, cover (right), 1 (right), 11, 13, 15, 25, 27; IgorGolovniov/Shutterstock Images, 4, 29; Petar Paunchev/Shutterstock Images, 7; Dmitry Eagle Orlov/Shutterstock Images, 8; rj lerich/Shutterstock Images, 16–17; Artem Mishukov/Shutterstock Images, 18; Jamie Hooper/Shutterstock Images, 21; sculpies/iStockphoto, 22

Library of Congress Cataloging-in-Publication Data
Library of Congress Cataloging-in-Publication Data is available on the Library of Congress website.

ISBN
978-1-64493-031-1 (hardcover)
978-1-64493-110-3 (paperback)
978-1-64493-268-1 (ebook pdf)
978-1-64493-189-9 (hosted ebook)

Printed in the United States of America
Mankato, MN
012020

About the Author

Sue Gagliardi writes fiction, nonfiction, and poetry for children. Her books include *Fairies*, *Get Outside in Winter*, and *Get Outside in Spring*. Her work appears in children's magazines including *Highlights Hello*, *Highlights High Five*, *Ladybug*, and *Spider*. She teaches kindergarten and lives in Pennsylvania with her husband and son.

Table of Contents

Chapter 1

The Three Little Pigs

A hungry wolf was looking for food. He came to the houses of three little pigs. The first house was made of straw. The wolf tried to get in. But the pig who lived there would not open the door.

 One pig put a lot of care into his house.

The wolf huffed and puffed. He blew down the straw house.

The pig ran to his brother's house. It was made of sticks. The wolf huffed and puffed. He blew down the stick house, too.

The two pigs ran to their brother's house. It was made of bricks. The wolf huffed and puffed with all his might. But he could not blow down the brick house. He decided to go down the chimney instead. But the pigs had a plan. They put a pot of

 The three little pigs had to outsmart the hungry wolf.

hot water under the chimney. The

wolf fell in. The pigs were safe.

Chapter 2

Build a Model House

The three little pigs needed a strong house to stay safe. Now it's your turn to build a house for them. The house should have a **foundation**, a roof, and four walls. The house should be windproof.

 In the fairy tale, only the brick house remained standing.

It should be strong enough that it does not fall down in the wind. It should also be large enough to hold all three pigs.

Materials

- Craft sticks
- Index cards
- Wooden blocks
- Tape or pipe cleaners
- Masking tape
- Ruler or tape measure
- Wind source (large fan or hair dryer)

- 3 toy pigs or other small figures

- Pen and paper

- Stopwatch

Instructions

Making the Houses

1. Use craft sticks to build the first **model** house. Make sure the three toys can fit inside. Attach the sticks together with tape or pipe cleaners.

2. Use index cards to build the second model house. Make sure

Habitat for Humanity is a group that builds new houses for people in need.

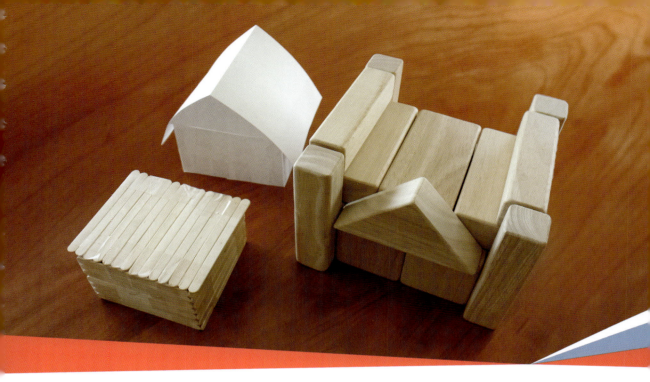

 This image shows a sample design for each house. Your houses could look very different.

the three toys can fit inside. Attach the index cards together with tape.

3. Use wooden blocks to build the third model house. Make sure the three toys can fit inside.

Testing the Houses

1. Use masking tape on the floor to make a starting line. Clear the floor of other objects.

2. Place the first house at the starting line.

3. Set up a wind source in front of the house. Ask an adult for help.

In England, some people live in cottages with thatched roofs. The roofs of the cottages are made from grass.

4. Turn the wind source on.

5. Measure how far the house moves. Record the distance. Measure how long the house stands. Record the time.

6. Repeat these steps for the other two houses.

Dome Homes

Most homes have straight walls and roofs. But some homes have a dome shape. They are shaped like half of a ball.

An igloo is a type of dome home made of blocks of snow. Its dome shape forms an arch. This curved shape makes the home strong. Other dome homes are built from a single block. People build the homes out of concrete.

The dome shape makes these houses stronger than typical homes. It spreads out the houses' weight evenly. Dome homes can withstand strong winds. They can protect people during hurricanes and tornadoes.

Dome homes can still have rectangular doors and windows.

Chapter 3

Results

The wooden blocks provide a strong base for the house. The index card house can be blown down more easily. The paper materials aren't as strong as the wood materials.

 People have been building with wood for more than 10,000 years.

Consider ways to make your houses stronger. Here are some ideas to try:

- Use modeling clay to **reinforce** the building materials.

- Make houses out of different shapes. Test which shapes create the strongest house.

Fun Fact

Builders use shapes such as triangles and arches to make stronger houses.

 Builders can put many triangles together to create a strong structure.

- Make shorter or taller houses. Which houses are stronger?

- Use new materials. What other materials could you use to build your houses?

Chapter 4

The Science of Strong Buildings

Engineers must consider **center of gravity** when designing buildings. An object's center of gravity is the point where its weight is balanced. A building with a center of gravity near its top may be top-heavy.

 Stable structures can last thousands of years.

The building could topple due to the uneven weight at the top.

In a **stable** building, the weight is evenly spread out. The center of gravity is near the center of the building. The building is less likely to fall over.

Every building needs a strong foundation. A foundation supports the whole building. It is like the roots of a tree. It keeps the building from sinking into the ground. A wide foundation spreads out the

CENTER OF GRAVITY

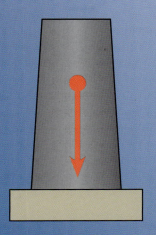

In a stable structure, the center of gravity is directly above its base. Beams or columns support the building's center of gravity.

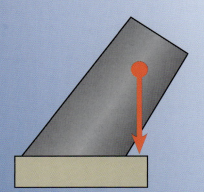

In an unstable structure, the center of gravity is not above the base. It is unsupported. The building will fall.

weight of the building. It makes the building more stable. It also brings the building's center of gravity closer to the ground.

Different **forces** can affect and damage buildings. External forces come from outside a building. High winds are one example. Internal forces come from within a building. **Tension** is one example. Engineers must consider these forces.

Steel, stones, and bricks are good building materials. They can hold

Fun Fact

Compression is an internal force. It presses materials together.

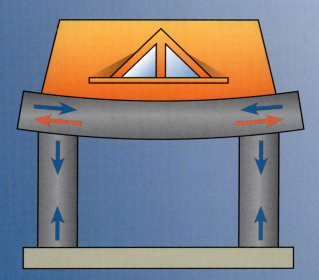

In buildings, beams that stand upright experience compression. The weight of the roof presses straight down on them. It squeezes them and makes them shorter. Horizontal beams experience both compression and tension. The weight of the roof causes the beams to bend a little. The tops of the beams squeeze smaller. But the bottoms of the beams stretch longer.

up against strong forces. Other materials such as cement help reinforce the building. The three little pigs are safest in a house made of these strong materials.

Making a Windproof House

Write your answers on a separate piece of paper.

1. Write a paragraph describing why engineers consider center of gravity when designing a building.

2. Why do you think it's important to test different models when building something?

3. How does a wide foundation make a building more stable?

   A. A wide foundation makes the building weigh more.

   B. A wide foundation spreads out the weight of a building.

   C. A wide foundation makes the building weigh less.

4. How is a foundation like the roots of a tree?

    A. Both provide support.

    B. Both are narrow.

    C. Both are wide.

5. What does **withstand** mean in this book?

*Dome homes can **withstand** strong winds. They can protect people during hurricanes and tornadoes.*

    A. become weaker than

    B. cause damage to

    C. stand up against

6. What does **topple** mean in this book?

*A building with a center of gravity near its top may be top-heavy. The building could **topple** due to the uneven weight at the top.*

    A. grow taller

    B. stand strong

    C. fall over

Answer key on page 32.

Glossary

center of gravity
The average center of all of an object's weight.

compression
A force that causes objects to squeeze together or causes a single object to become more compact.

forces
Pushes or pulls that happen when one object interacts with another object.

foundation
The supporting base of a structure.

model
A small copy of a real object.

reinforce
To support or make stronger.

stable
Unlikely to move, break, or change.

tension
A pulling force that stretches materials apart.

To Learn More

BOOKS

Enz, Tammy. *Structural Engineering: Learn It, Try It!* North Mankato, MN: Capstone Press, 2018.

Swanson, Jennifer. *Explore Forces and Motion!* White River Junction, VT: Nomad Press, 2016.

Westing, Jemma. *Out of the Box*. New York: DK Publishing, 2017.

NOTE TO EDUCATORS

Visit **www.focusreaders.com** to find lesson plans, activities, links, and other resources related to this title.

Index

C
center of gravity, 23–25
compression, 26–27

D
dome homes, 16

F
forces, 26–27
foundation, 9, 24

H
Habitat for Humanity, 12

P
pigs, 5–7, 9–11, 27

R
roofs, 9, 14, 16, 27

S
shapes, 16, 20

T
tension, 26–27

W
wolf, 5–7